TWENTY

SPINE TINGLING

MINI MYSTERIES

Scholastic Children's Books,
Scholastic Publications Ltd,
7-9 Pratt Street, London NW1 0AE, UK

Scholastic Inc.,
730 Broadway, New York, NY 10003, USA

Scholastic Canada Ltd,
123 Newkirk Road, Richmond Hill,
Ontario, Canada L4C 3G5

Ashton Scholastic Pty Ltd,
PO Box 579, Gosford, New South Wales,
Australia

Ashton Scholastic Ltd,
Private Bag 1, Penrose, Auckland,
New Zealand

First published by Scholastic Publications Ltd, 1993
Text copyright © Dina Anastasio, 1993
Illustrations copyright © Kim Blundell, 1993

ISBN: 0 590 55325 9

Printed by Cox & Wyman Ltd, Reading, Berks

Dina Anastasio

TWENTY

SPINE

TINGLING

MINI
MYSTERIES

Illustrated by Kim Blundell

Hippo

CONTENTS

1
**One Sausage Pizza, Two Pieces
with Mushrooms 13**

2
The Case of the Horrible Fingerprint 18

3

The Thirteenth Floor   24

4

The Goldfish   29

5

A Night on the Big Wheel   35

6

The Spider that Wouldn't Die   42

7

The Tap on the Window 49

8

The Scavenger Hunt 53

9

The Mind Reader 61

10

The Secret Room 65

11
The Mystery of the Ghostly Footsteps 72

12
The Horror Film 78

13
The Thing 82

14
The Howling 88

15

The Dummy 94

16

The Ghostly Message 102

17

Lost! 107

18

The House of Horrors 113

19
The Cave 120

20
The Ghost of Greenfield Manor 127

Answers 133

Dear Detective,

Welcome to the murky world of spine tingling mini mysteries. There are twenty mysteries in this book for you to solve. Read each story carefully, then try and work out the answer. You can check your answers in the ANSWERS section at the back of the book.

Good hunting.

1. ONE SAUSAGE PIZZA, TWO PIECES WITH MUSHROOMS

It was going to be a long night, and all four of them were very hungry. They would order pizza, just like they always did, and they would eat it while they watched television, just like they always did. Then they would climb up to the attic with their sleeping bags, and whisper scary stories all night long.

And they would all order sausage on their pizzas, just like they always did.

At six o'clock, Suzi dialled the pizza place and ordered "One large sausage pizza." But, this time, as she was about to hang up the phone, a very strange thing happened. Anita said, "Ask them to put mushrooms on my two pieces." And Suzi did.

At seven o'clock the pizza still had not been delivered, and the girls were edgy with hunger. Suzi called again.

"The delivery man went out to you," said the voice on the phone. "But he got sick and came right back. I'm sending another man."

Suzi hung up the phone, and went into the living room. The other girls were watching television.

The pizza arrived ten minutes later. Suzi paid the man, placed the pizza box on the table in the kitchen, and went back to the television. During the commercial, Anne went to the lavatory, and when she came back, Minnie went too. Then they all went into the kitchen and Suzi opened the box.

Something was very wrong. Instead of eight pieces there were only seven. Six had sausages on them, and one was covered with sausages *and* mushrooms. The second sausage and mushroom piece was missing.

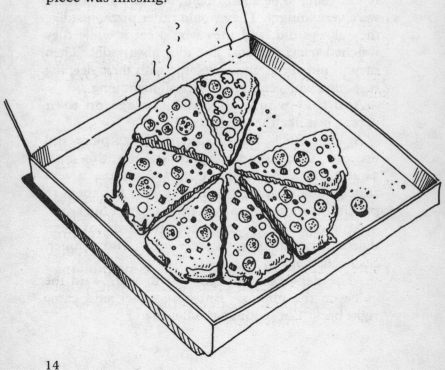

Now Anita was a nice girl, and so she tried very hard not to complain. But everyone knew she was disappointed.

"That's a terrible thing to do," Anne said. "No one should take another person's piece of pizza. I know I'd never do anything like that."

"Me either," said Suzi.

"Me either," said Minnie.

Anita didn't say anything. She just sat down at the table with the others and took one bite of her second piece. It was cold. She couldn't eat it.

She leaned over, tossed the rest of the slice into the cat's dish, and went back into the living room.

The girls spent the next hour watching television. Anita stared at the screen, but she couldn't really concentrate. She kept thinking about that first slice of pizza. Where was it? What had happened to it? *Had* one of her friends eaten it, and if so, which one?

15

The last programme was just finishing when the cat crawled in. Suzi noticed her first. She looked odd, somehow. Her eyes seemed strangely glazed and her back sagged. She was clearly ill.

Minnie went to her and stroked her and said, "She looks awful, doesn't she?"

As the girls watched, the cat grew more and more miserable, until she couldn't stand. Suzi called the vet.

"What's she eaten?" the vet asked.

"Nothing much," Suzi said. "Just some pizza with sausage and mushrooms."

"Ahh," said the vet. "Mushrooms. Mushrooms can be very dangerous. Watch her and if she gets worse call me. If she isn't very, very sick by morning then the mushrooms are all right and she'll be fine."

The girls watched the cat, and then they watched each other. And they were all thinking: *I wonder who ate that other piece of pizza?*

The cat grew worse and the vet came and took her away. When they were gone, Anita said, "Whoever ate my pizza had better own up so that we can call a doctor."

Three heads shook back and forth, back and forth. "Not me," they said. "Not me." "Not me." Then who?

They sat there together as the sun went down and the room filled with menacing shadowy shapes. No one spoke. They just sat there without moving and stared at each other, and waited, and waited.

They waited there all night: waited for one of the shadows to fall to the ground, waited and watched and waited.

By morning they were all very tired, but no one had become ill.

"I don't understand," Anita said, as she got ready to go home. "Whatever happened to my slice of pizza?"

"I think I know," Suzi said. "Yes, as a matter of fact, I'm sure I know."

Do you?

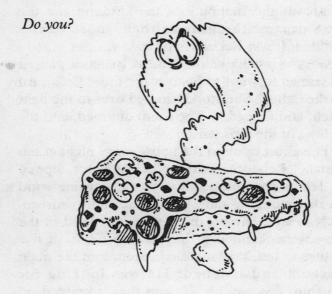

2. THE CASE OF THE HORRIBLE FINGERPRINT

The storm was growing now. Outside, the world shook and groaned as the wind and the rain pounded the old house. But inside, the only sound was the snapping of the kindling and the soft voices of the girls as their ghost stories unfolded. It was Rebecca's turn.

"Wait," Camilia whispered, as Rebecca paused and leaned forward to poke at the fire. "Let's turn out the lights." She stood, tiptoed over to the light switch, and flipped it. The room dimmed, and the shadows of the girls tensed.

"The ghost came to the house every night at ten o'clock," Rebecca continued. Her voice dipped and fell as she competed with the howling wind and the pounding rain. "He came softly, unseen, barely heard. At first, the people who lived in the house were terrified of him. Every night, at five minutes to ten, they huddled together in the main bedroom and listened. He was looking for something. As we, uh, I mean they, trembled on the big bed, he opened drawers, slammed closet doors, and moved furniture around below. He came every night, at exactly ten o'clock, but he never seemed to find what he was looking for."

"You said 'we'," Janet murmured.

Rebecca hesitated, as the old house creaked and hummed around her. No one spoke. No one moved. The only sound was the *snap snap, snap,* of Jane's chewing gum.

"Can't you stop that?" Camilia demanded angrily. "It interferes with the atmosphere."

"I can't," Jane said. "You know I'm always chewing gum, and I always snap it. That's just what I do."

"Shhh," Rebecca said. "Anyway, it was this house. It was this house, and the people huddling together on the bed were this family. It was me. I heard him... no, I hear him, I still hear him, every single night, at exactly ten o'clock."

The girls pulled back, waited, wondered.

"Who is he?"

"What does he want?"

"We think he lived here a long time ago," Rebecca whispered. "We think he must have been a seaman of some kind because once, on a very dark, cold, wet night, we heard him humming a tune, softly, over and over and over, and it was a song of the sea. We know what he wants. He wants his charm, his lucky charm. I finally found it, late last night, after he had gone away. It's over there, on the table under the window. I put it there so that he'll find it when he comes tonight. Shhh....."

From somewhere far away came the echo of a church bell chiming once.

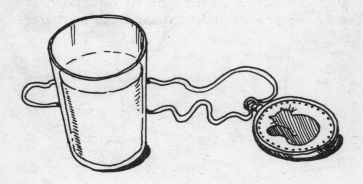

"It's a quarter to ten," Rebecca said. "He'll be here soon. We'd better put the fire out. He needs complete darkness, or he won't come." She pulled herself up, and flipped on the light.

The charm was there, on the table, waiting for him. Beside it was a glass of juice. Rebecca had put it there, "Just in case he's thirsty from his journey."

Rebecca doused the fire, gathered the girls behind the sofa, turned off the light, and joined them.

The girls were blinded now by the blackness. They could not see anything, not even each other, but they could hear; and what they heard, as the bells chimed ten, was something falling, breaking, shattering, followed by the sound of someone, something, moving about.

"It's him," Rebecca whispered. "It's the ghost."

And then he was gone, and the room was quiet again. Even the storm had abated, and outside the world was silent, too.

Rebecca turned on the light. It was the glass that had broken – and the charm: the lucky charm was gone.

"Wait a minute," Rebecca whispered. "It was just a story. I made it up. I've never heard a ghost, not really. That was *my* charm, my *lucky* charm. So what happened to it? We're the only ones here, so one of you must have taken it."

Each of the girls, in turn, denied taking the charm, but Rebecca didn't believe them. And that was when Rebecca noticed the fingerprint.

It was horrible.

It was bloody.

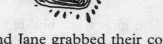

It was huge.

It was so terrible, in fact, that Camilia and Jane grabbed their coats and ran home.

Rebecca called them the following morning and asked them to come back. "I couldn't sleep," she said when they arrived. "I was up half the night thinking about that horrible bloody print. Ghosts don't have fingerprints. Ghosts don't bleed. This fingerprint belongs to one of you!"

She led them then, across the room and over to the table. The huge, bloody print was still there.

She examined their fingers, one at a time, for cuts. They both had them, and they both had explanations as to how they got the cuts. Then they placed their fingers in the horrible, bloody, huge fingerprint. But it was so smudged, and distorted, that it proved nothing.

There were other fingerprints too, horrible, bloody fingerprints, leading downward, down the tabletop, and under it.

"I thought about those fingerprints all night long," Rebecca said. "Why would there be fingerprints leading down, down, and under the table?"

"Maybe somebody wanted to hide something," Camilia suggested. "And come back for it later."

"Like a charm," Rebecca said.

"How could anyone hide a charm under a tabletop?" Jane asked.

"There's only one way," Rebecca said.

"I'm stuck," Camilia said.

"And so was my charm," said Rebecca, holding it up for everyone to see. "I found it last night. The bloody fingerprints led me there."

One of the girls hid the charm under the tabletop. Do you know who it was? How did she fix it there?

3. THE THIRTEENTH FLOOR

Sophie and Tim stepped into the lift and waited as the door slid shut. They were on their way to visit their uncle.

"Which floor?" Tim asked.

"Eighteen, I think."

Tim pushed the eighteen button and leaned against the back of the lift. The car began to bang and creak and move slowly, slowly upward.

"This lift's really shaky and noisy – and very slow," Sophie said.

Tim shrugged. "It's an old building," he said. "Old buildings have old lifts."

Sophie looked up. There was no number thirteen on the light-up indicator panel.

"I've heard that some buildings don't have thirteenth floors," she said. "Lots of people think that the number thirteen is unlucky, so they think nobody wants to live there. I suppose this building's like that."

Tim pointed to the numbers on the buttons that you push.

"There's a thirteen button here," he said. "See."

"Push it," Sophie said.

But Tim didn't think it was such a good idea. "What if it stops at thirteen?" he said.

"It can't. If it stops at thirteen, then the thirteen light up there will have to light up, and there is no thirteen light up there, so it can't."

"All right, I'm going to push it," Tim said. And he did.

The lift squeaked and shivered and then it jolted to a stop – at twelve.

"Push it again," Sophie said.

This time the lift jolted to a stop at fourteen. "See?" Tim said. "There is no thirteenth floor."

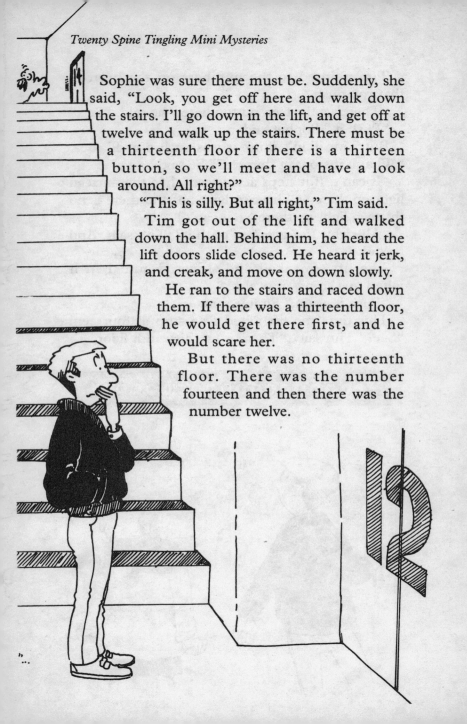

Sophie was sure there must be. Suddenly, she said, "Look, you get off here and walk down the stairs. I'll go down in the lift, and get off at twelve and walk up the stairs. There must be a thirteenth floor if there is a thirteen button, so we'll meet and have a look around. All right?"

"This is silly. But all right," Tim said.

Tim got out of the lift and walked down the hall. Behind him, he heard the lift doors slide closed. He heard it jerk, and creak, and move on down slowly.

He ran to the stairs and raced down them. If there was a thirteenth floor, he would get there first, and he would scare her.

But there was no thirteenth floor. There was the number fourteen and then there was the number twelve.

He could hear the lift creaking, and rattling, and shaking.

Tim stopped and listened. The lift was still creaking steadily, slowly, downwards.

Tim opened the door to the twelfth floor and looked down the corridor. It looked just like any other floor to him. The lift was jerking to a stop now. He heard it squeak and then he heard it stop.

He slammed the stairwell door shut and crouched down to wait for Sophie. Maybe he should just wait there in the stairwell and scare her when she arrived. Yes, maybe that's what he'd do.

And then he heard her coming down the hall on the twelfth floor. She opened the door to the stairs, and when she came towards him, Tim jumped out with a yell. Sophie screamed.

But she recovered soon enough and in a minute she was able to talk. This is what she said:

"There *is* a thirteenth floor," she said. "And I've been there. There are cobwebs all over the place, and the doors are hanging off their hinges, and I heard footsteps pacing and pacing. Ghosts were sighing behind the doors of the flats and rats were scurrying around everywhere. Things in white robes were fluttering about all over the place... and – "

"Sophie," Tim said, interrupting her.

"Hmmm?"

"How did you say you got into this floor?"

"On the lift," Sophie said. "I pushed the thirteen button, and this time the door opened."

"And how did you get back down *here*?"

"On the lift, of course," Sophie said. "I just pushed the button and the lift arrived and I came down here to twelve. I was going to walk up to fourteen and find you."

"Sophie," Tim said. "You're lying."

How did Tim know that?

4. THE GOLDFISH

The sound of Mark's voice echoed through the house.

"*Where's my goldfish?*" he hollered.

"Where did you leave it?" his mother called.

"In the bath, of course," Mark whined. "I filled up the bath and put my goldfish in it, and now it's gone. I bet Sally took it. She liked it, so I bet she's got it somewhere in her room."

Mark went into Sally's room. Sally was sitting on her bed over in the corner.

"Where's my goldfish?" Mark asked.

Sally was trying to pretend that he wasn't there. She was fingering the damp cuff of her long-sleeved shirt and shaking her bare feet.

"Where's my goldfish, Sally?" Mark shouted.

"Maybe it went down the drain."

Mark thought about that for a while and then he said, "That's impossible. The bath's still full."

"Well, maybe somebody let the water out, and the goldfish went down the drain, and they filled it up again. Now go away!"

Mark went away. He went into the bathroom, pulled out the plug, and ran a hot bath for himself. Then he climbed in, lay back, and closed his eyes.

After a while he opened his eyes again and looked straight ahead. Something was watching him from behind those six little holes in the silver overflow. It was something with big yellowish eyes.

Mark wondered if it was his goldfish. But how would his goldfish have found its way up there behind that drain? Wouldn't she have floated *down* the drain?

The yellow eyes kept watching him.

The water was getting cold now. He should put more hot water in. But what if it went into the overflow and washed his goldfish away?

Mark decided to take the silver piece off the overflow and rescue his fish.

First he got out of the bath. Then he dried himself. Then he put his clothes back on. And then he prised the drain off.

The goldfish was gone.

Mark turned away, then turned back and looked at the hole where the drain cover had been.

Suddenly a long furry leg slid out of the overflow, and then another, and another, and another. The legs were followed by the yellow eyes, and the fur and the body of a horrible, huge, furry...*SPIDER.*

Mark lept back, and froze. The spider moved about on the edge of the bath, but it kept looking at him with those strange yellowish eyes. I will get you, it seemed to say. I will get you just like I got your goldfish.

The furry legs moved towards him.

Mark stepped back. "What have you done with my goldfish?" he whispered. And then he said it louder, and louder, and louder still. "*WHAT HAVE YOU DONE WITH MY GOLDFISH?*"

Mark sighed. There was nothing to be done. His goldfish was gone, forever. Now he must dispose of this creature, this murderer.

But how?

Suddenly Mark had an idea.

He closed the bathroom door and went to get a broom.

When he came back, the spider was still there, tiptoing around and around the bath, waiting for him.

He raised the broom and slid it behind the spider. Then he pushed it into the water.

The spider kept moving, and it kept watching Mark.

Now came the tricky part. He would have to reach in there and pull out the plug. He waited. He waited for a long time, until it was at the back end of the bath, and then he shoved his sleeve down into the water and pulled out the plug.

The water went out, and the spider went with it. And as it went, Mark thought about his goldfish and he felt sad.

He went into his room and tried to do his homework, but all he could think about was his goldfish. His goldfish was *inside* that horrible spider, gurgling down, down, down, through the drainpipes.

Or was she? Suddenly Mark remembered something. He remembered shoving his arm into the bath water, pulling the plug, and watching the spider disappear.

His goldfish wasn't inside the spider after all. It was inside something else, and it was probably a goldfish bowl.

Mark went into his sister's room. "Give me back my goldfish," he said. "I know you took it."

"How did you know?" Sally asked, as she went to her wardrobe and brought out a goldfish bowl.

Mark smiled. "I knew when I looked at you that you had something up your sleeve."

Then he took his goldfish back to his room.

How could Mark tell that Sally had taken the goldfish?

5. A NIGHT ON THE BIG WHEEL

Angela and Edmond Desmond ran through the amusement park and skidded to a stop in front of the big wheel ticket booth.

"Good!" Angela said as she caught her breath. "We're the first ones. Now we'll get the best seat."

"All the seats are the same, aren't they?" Edmond asked. "I mean, it's a circle, after all."

Angela shrugged and gave the money to the man behind the counter. Then she led her younger brother through the gate and into the seat at the bottom of the wheel. When they were locked in, the seat swung gently, back and forth, back and forth, as the wheel began to rise above the park.

When it was halfway to the top, it jerked and came to a stop.

"What's happening?" Edmond asked nervously.

"Look down," his sister said. "A man is getting on."

Edmond unsquinted his eyes and glanced down over his left shoulder. A very tall, very thin man was settling into the car nearest the ground.

A few minutes later the wheel began to move again. It turned slowly, slowly, then stopped.

"What's happening now?" Edmond whispered.

"Open your eyes, Edmond!" Angela said.

Edmond opened his eyes and looked. They were at the very top now. Edmond closed his eyes again.

"Look, Edmond," Angela cried. "A man in a very strange red hat is getting on." As she said this she moved, and the car swung back and forth again.

"Stop that!" Edmond cried, as the wheel began to turn once more. They stopped one more time, halfway between the top and the bottom, and a short fat man got on. When he was settled the wheel began to turn, and turn, and turn, until, at last, it stopped again.

"Now what?" Edmond asked. His eyes were still closed, and his voice was so soft and tense that his sister barely heard him.

"They're letting someone off, Edmond," Angela sighed.

"Us?"

"Not yet. We're halfway up."

After a moment the wheel began to move again, but for some reason it didn't stop when Angela and Edmond reached the top. It kept right on going, then stopped when they were halfway down.

"We'll be next, then," Edmond whispered, as the wheel turned again. But it didn't stop when they were at the bottom. Instead, the boy who was running it just grinned a mean grin and waved, and up they went again.

"That's funny," Edmond said as they moved back up again. "There's nobody around. Nobody at all. Do you think they've all gone home?"

"There's someone else to get off yet," said Angela.

They stopped at the top.

"Is he getting out?" Edmond asked.

"I don't know. I don't think I want to look."

"Why not?"

"Because I'm scared, Edmond. OK?" Angela sounded more annoyed than scared, and Edmond didn't speak again for several minutes.

"Angela?" he said. He was grasping the bar so that it wouldn't move.

"Hmmm?"

"The lights are going out. See, there's nobody here. Maybe they're closing the park."

Angela opened her eyes and looked. All the lights in the park were out and there was no one around – no one at all. It was dusk now. Soon it would be dark.

And the wheel wasn't moving.

Angela leaned over and looked down. All the cars were empty, and the boy who was running the machine was gone. No, *no*, he was there: over there, lying on the ground. His hands and his feet were tied up and around his mouth there was a gag.

Angela sat back up and stared at her little brother, her eyes filled with terror. "Edmond," she whispered. "Somebody's tied up the guy who runs this thing, and so now he can't run it any more, and..."

"And we have to stay here until morning."

Angela nodded and held the bar tighter, but it was getting windy now and the car began to rock.

Angela and Edmond held the bar tighter and stared straight ahead. There were no lights in the park at all now. Everyone was gone. They were alone.

There was no moon that night, and as the sky grew darker and darker they could not even see each other.

The car rocked harder, then harder and harder, as the wind came up, until it was swinging up and down like a ship in forty-foot waves.

"Stop!" Edmond screamed. "Stop! *Stop!*"

But Angela wasn't doing anything so she could not stop it from swaying. Both of them were crying now. They knew that this could go on for hours and hours, until morning came.

And then the thunder began. At first it was far away, but before long it rolled closer and closer.

There was no lightning, so maybe the storm wouldn't happen, Angela thought. But what if the lightning *did* come? What would they do then? They were way up there, on top of the world. The lightning would be sure to strike them up there.

"Should we climb down?" Angela said.

"No."

"What do you mean, no?"

"It's too far. We might fall."

And of course he was right. If they had started to climb through the darkness they would almost certainly fall. They would just have to wait there.

Just before dawn the thunder rolled away. Soon

the sun came up, as it always does. Angela and Edmond wiped the tears from their eyes and looked at each other. Someone would come soon and rescue them. Below them, the man was still there, with his hands and feet tied, and his mouth gagged.

Two workmen arrived at eight and they called the police, who brought Angela and Edmond down, and when they were safe the police asked them questions.

"The man was robbed," the police said. "Did you see who did it?"

Angela and Edmond shook their heads. "We didn't look," they said. "We didn't look."

But then Angela thought very hard, and suddenly she remembered something, and she said "*Wait*. I *do* know who did it."

Do you?

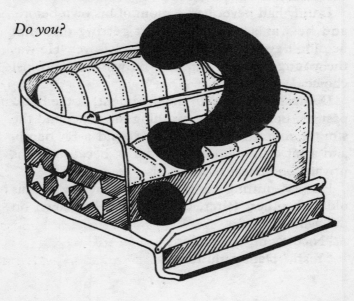

6. THE SPIDER THAT WOULDN'T DIE

Danny O'Brien hadn't wanted to move until he saw the big house on the hill, and then he couldn't wait. It was enormous. It had six bedrooms, one for Mr and Mrs O'Brien, and one for each of the five children.

Danny had never had a room of his own before, and he was so excited about getting one that he didn't even mind that it was a leftover. He was the youngest, after all, and he was used to last choice.

Danny's room was in the basement, at the back, past the boiler, and the washing machine, and the storage room. It was a bit cold, and a bit damp, and a bit clammy; but he loved it, because it was private, and because it was his.

He was putting his books on a shelf when his oldest brother, Peter, came in and lay down on the bed.

"Nice room," Peter said.

"Yeah," Danny muttered.

"It's better than I thought, now that the shelves are up."

Danny didn't say anything. He just kept stacking the books, but he knew what was coming.

"You've got the best room in the house, Danny Boy," Peter said. "How come you've got the best room in the house when you're so little?"

I knew it, Danny thought. I *knew* it. I knew it. Every time I get something nice, *he* wants it. But this time he's not going to get it, not if I can help it.

"Pity about the spider," Peter said, as he hugged Danny's pillow and rolled over onto his side.

Now, if there was one thing that Danny hated and feared more than anything in the world it was spiders. He hated the way they crept around without making a sound. He hated all those legs tiptoeing about, scurrying from here to there, all furry and silent. So, when Peter said that about the spider, Danny's back tensed and his neck began to sweat, and his body started to tremble.

Behind him, Peter was beginning to chuckle, very, very softly.

He wants my room, Danny thought. Now that it's mine, he wants it – but he isn't going to get it, no matter how much he talks about spiders.

"Up there, in the corner," Peter said. "See."

Peter was right. There *was* a spider there, in the corner above the door.

Danny stepped back, then stepped forward again. He wouldn't let Peter have it, not this time. He liked his new room too much to let Peter have it. It was only a little spider, wasn't it? Nothing at all to be afraid of. Spiders didn't hurt people, did they? Anyway, this spider was so busy building its web that it wasn't interested in Danny.

"I'm not scared," he said, straightening his shoulders and glaring down at his big brother.

But of course he *was* scared.
He was very, very scared. That
night he slept with the light on
and he hardly slept at all. He
kept watching the spider tiptoe up
and down those tiny sticky threads of
its web.

The next morning Danny couldn't eat his
breakfast. He picked at his cereal, and could only
drink one tiny sip of juice before he felt sick and
had to return to his room and lie down. He lay
there for a long time before he found the nerve to
look up at the corner.

The spider was bigger. Its hairy legs were longer
than they had been, and its disgusting furry body
was rounder, and fatter, and... and it was growing!

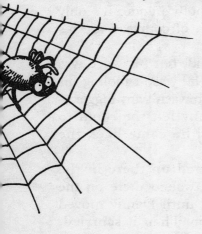

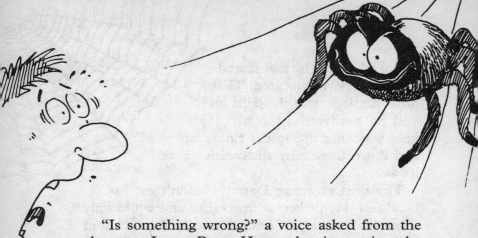

"Is something wrong?" a voice asked from the doorway. It was Peter. He was leaning against the door jamb, grinning that mean little grin that he always grinned when he was trying to get at his little brother.

"No," Danny said. "Nothing's wrong. Nothing at all. Where is everybody?"

"Out," Peter said. "Everybody's gone. It's only you, and me, and the spider, of course. I see it's grown."

"I don't mind," Danny said, but his voice was trembling and he knew that he wasn't fooling his brother at all. At least the web wasn't any bigger.

A few minutes later Danny left the room to brush his teeth, and when he came back the spider was bigger still.

Its hairy furry body bulged up there in the corner. Its eight skinny legs waited there on the clean whiteness of the wall, until Danny moved into the far corner in terror. Then it scurried, scurried, down the wall, and across the floor, towards him.

Danny screamed and ran from the room.

Peter was out there, waiting, grinning that mean grin again, and when he heard the scream he chuckled and said, "You could always give the room to me – if you're afraid of spiders, that is."

Danny said that he wasn't afraid at all, and he certainly wasn't going to give his room up, ever. Then he went upstairs to see if his parents had come home yet. They hadn't.

When he came back, Peter was lying on the bed, pointing to the spider. It was back in the corner, and now it was twice the size it had been ten minutes before. It looked huge on that little web.

It was horrifying. It was repulsive. It was huge! It was the biggest, most terrifying thing that Danny had ever, ever seen.

Its round, swollen eyes followed Danny as he shrank into the far corner. "Give up your room," it seemed to say. "Give it up. Give it up."

"*No!*" Danny cried. "You *cannot* have my room!"

Peter chuckled and pointed to the thing in the corner.

"I guess you like your room-mate, then," he whispered. "At the rate he's growing, there won't be any... room... for... *you*... soon."

Something's wrong, Danny thought. I know. I know! That's it! That spider wasn't growing at all. It was a different spider. Peter put it there. Peter put them all there. It had been a different spider every time. If it had been the same spider as the one in the beginning, then something else would have grown too. Wouldn't it?

That night Danny's father took the spider out into the woods and left it there. Danny slept soundly that night, in his own basement room.

What else would have grown if the spider had been the same every time?

7. THE TAP ON THE WINDOW

Darkness engulfed him. It was there, everywhere, as the boy opened his eyes and tried to understand where he was.

He realized, slowly, slowly, as he came awake, that he was in his bed. He could feel that this was his pillow, his blanket, his room.

He rolled over and tried to remember. That tapping, that strange tapping, it had been part of his dream, hadn't it? Hadn't it? Or had it been real? In the dream someone had been outside his window. No, no, it wasn't someone at all. It was some *thing*, signalling him to come out: now, *now*, hurry. Something wanted him, desperately wanted him to come out – or maybe he – it – wanted to come in.

It had been a dream. Hadn't it?

The next night he decided that he would stay awake. He would know then, once and for all, if there was someone out there, tapping, tapping, tapping.

He sat up in his bed all night and waited. He
heard nothing, nothing at all. But towards dawn
he fell asleep again, and when he awoke again
inside that blackness he remembered the tapping,
tapping, but he could not tell if the tapping had
come from outside the window or if it had been
part of that strange dream.

Hard as he tried, he could not stay awake for a
whole night, so he decided to tape it. That would do
it. If the tapping was real, he would have it on tape.

The next night he closed all the windows in the
room and locked them from the inside. Then he
set up his tape recorder, placed it on the floor
beneath the window by his bed, and fell asleep.

He awoke early the next morning, pushed the play button – and heard it.

The tapping was real. *Tap, tap, tap, tap,* never changing, always the same, *tap, tap, tap.* And then... something else... a scream, a horrible, terrified scream.

He pushed the rewind button and played it again, then again, and again, as he tried to remember where he had heard that voice before.

Of course. It was his own voice, his own scream, his own terror. *He* was screaming, screaming – but why? Was it the *something* on the other side of the window that was frightening him? Was it the *something* that was tapping?

The next time he played the tape he compared the sound of the scream and the sound of the tapping and he thought – no, he knew – that both were coming from inside the room. They were coming from inside *his* room. There had been something *in the room with him,* something that shouldn't have been there, something... in the darkness. He shivered.

That night he locked the door to his bedroom. Then he locked all the windows. And then he turned on the machine.

He dreamed about the horrible thing again, the horrible thing that came to his window and tapped for him to come out, come out, come out.

He awoke early and played the tape. There was that screaming again, his own horrible, terrifying screaming. And there was the tapping, tapping, tapping. It was clear. It was unmuffled. It was *inside the room.*

What was it? He rose from his bed, found his stick, and began to search the room, until he knew, at last, what had been tapping, tapping, tapping.

Do you know?

8. THE SCAVENGER HUNT

Jamie James was a strange boy who thought a lot about himself. On this particular occasion he was so busy thinking about himself that he barely heard his sister Sally say, "The scavenger hunt is about to begin."

"What?" Jamie asked dreamily.

"I said, 'The scavenger hunt is about to begin'," Sally repeated in an annoyed tone. Sally was often annoyed, probably because she was fourteen, and the oldest, and she always had to think of things for Jamie and the twins to do. "You know," she said, "in a scavenger hunt you get a list of things and you have to find them all. I've made up a list. We don't have very much time, so you'll only have to find four things. The first one who gets back here with all four things is the winner. Here's the list."

Sally handed a piece of paper to Jamie, and one to each of her twin sisters, Jill and Joleen.

On each of the lists were written the same four items.

1. A green hat.
2. A large flat rock that looks like a turtle's back.
3. A bone.
4. A mirror with a crack in it.

Sally had just thought of the four items a few minutes before. She hadn't hidden them. She had just written the words on the lists. She had chosen them because she thought they would be hard to find, and searching for them would keep everyone busy for a long time.

Jill and Joleen grabbed their lists and ran to the front door, but Jamie didn't move. He was too busy dreaming about becoming a superstar.

"Come *on,*" Sally urged him. "Don't you want to win?"

Jamie looked down at his paper, and then he stood up and joined his sisters by the front door.

Now there was a mirror near the front door that was just the right height for Jamie to look into if he stood on his tiptoes, and Jamie always looked into it when he passed. This time he stopped at it, and looked into it, and smiled. Then he took it down from the hook on the wall and looked at himself more closely.

"Hurry up!" Sally said from behind him, and so Jamie put the mirror back quickly, and waited as his sister said good-bye to their tiny dog.

"Goodbye, Lester," she said as she patted him. "We won't be long, and you'll be fine here by yourself."

When she had finished, and gone outside, Jamie slammed the door behind him, hard. He always slammed the door hard, but Jamie wasn't a very thoughtful person.

Then he wandered off to win the treasure hunt.

55

He found the green hat right away. It was sitting on the bonnet of an old lorry in the next street, and it was wonderful. It was all green, and it was kind of like a cowboy hat, and it was huge.

When he put it on his head it came way down over his eyes.

"That certainly was lucky," he said to himself.

The rock was harder. He looked for a long time, and then he saw one that looked just like a

turtle's back sticking out of the bottom of his neighbour's stone wall. He pulled it out and, as the wall teetered, he went on.

He found the bone a few minutes later. It was a huge beef bone, and it was partially buried under an apple tree down the road.

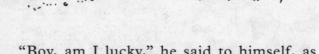

"Boy, am I lucky," he said to himself, as he slipped the bone into his other pocket.

Now he must find a cracked mirror. That would be very difficult indeed.

Of course, there was always that mirror by the front door at home. Maybe he could just crack that a little bit and then he would win. But didn't they say that to break a mirror meant seven years' bad luck? Did a crack count? Seven years was a very long time.

He didn't believe in silly superstitions like that, did he? Of course he didn't.

But what if it was true? He'd never be a superstar, would he? And he'd probably fail his history exam. He thought and he thought, but he couldn't think of anything else that was too terrible.

He turned and headed home.

He didn't think about the mirror again until he was coming up his path.

Jill and Joleen and Sally were standing by the front door. They all had green hats and rocks and bones, but they were all boring.

They hadn't even *found* their green hats. They had just taken their own hats before they went out: Jill and Joleen each had a winter woolly hat, and Sally's was velvet with a floppy brim, that she'd had for her birthday. And their rocks didn't even look like turtles' backs. He knew where they'd found them. They'd found them in the pile of rocks that their parents were going to use for the patio. And they had chicken bones... *chicken bones!* Last night's chicken bones that they had found in the rubbish. It was all too boring.

No one had found a mirror with a crack in it.

When Jamie saw that, he started thinking about the mirror by the front door again. He didn't believe in seven years of bad luck.

Those kind of things didn't really happen.

He'd just knock the mirror off the wall before the others had a chance to come inside, and maybe he'd just step on it a little, and then he'd win.

But Sally got to the door first. The others were right behind her, so when she saw the cracked mirror on the floor and gasped, everybody could see just what she was gasping about. And everybody was so busy gasping that they didn't even think about the treasure hunt....except for Jamie.

Jamie picked up the cracked mirror. While he was leaning over, Lester came and whined, and Sally examined his paw and found a sliver of glass there.

"I wonder who broke it," Sally said.

"Seven years' bad luck," Joleen whispered, a bit nervously.

"That's silly," Jamie said. "Anyway, I win the scavenger hunt."

Just then there was a knock on the front door, and a very large, very angry man came in.

The man folded his arms and glared down at Jamie. "That's my hat!" he shouted. He grabbed the green hat off of Jamie's head. "Where'd you find it?"

Before Jamie could answer, the neighbour arrived. "I saw you pull that rock out of my wall,

Jamie. You didn't even notice that a big chunk of it fell down. You'll have a lot of work to do this afternoon..."

And then the dog arrived. It was the biggest, fiercest, most terrible-looking dog that Jamie had ever seen. It burst through the door with its mouth wide open, leapt at Jamie and knocked him over, and tore at his pocket until it found the bone.

"Seven years of bad luck, Jamie," Sally whispered. "Seven terrible, horrible years."

"But I didn't break it," Jamie moaned. "It was cracked when I picked it up."

"But you did," his sister said. "I know you did. No one else could have. Just think of it, you'll be seventeen when all those awful, horrible things stop happening."

Jamie did break the mirror. Can you guess how it happened?

9. THE MIND READER

Sandy slid down in her chair and waited for the mind reader. She hoped that the mind reader wouldn't come. Her friend Jill had said, "Sandy, please come to the mind reader with me." And Sandy had said, "Sure I'll come." But that was a month ago. Now she wished she hadn't agreed to it.

Sandy closed her eyes and took a deep breath. She was scared. She was scared because yesterday she had committed her first real crime and now she was about to sit in front of a psychic who might be able to read her mind.

There was nothing to do but pretend that she was somewhere else. That way the mind reader wouldn't know what she was thinking.

Sandy felt terrible about taking the watch, especially since it belonged to her uncle and it was brand new. It was so brand new in fact that no one but Sandy and her uncle had ever seen it. But it had looked so tempting lying there by the sink.

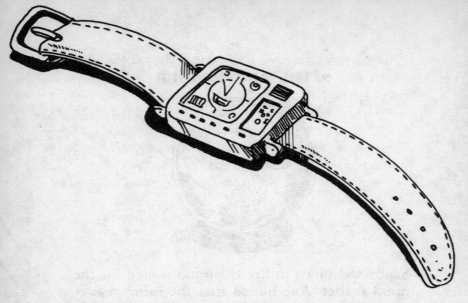

It had a microphone in it, and a tiny computer, and it played microscopic tapes and it reminded you of things, like what time it was in Moscow and Brazil and what you had to do that day. And all the numbers on it were different colours.

Who could resist a watch like that?

Now here she was, and the only thing in her mind was the wonderful watch in her right pocket. She was very, very scared, especially since her uncle had decided to come with her to the mind reader at the last minute.

Where was Jill? She was late. Jill was always late these days. Ever since she'd started that mysterious new job, she wasn't even a friend. She was always too busy to listen. When Sandy told her about the watch she hadn't paid attention, and when she showed it to her she barely looked at it.

The mind reader was walking onto the stage now, and taking a chair, and sitting, and thinking, and looking out into the audience.

The mind reader was staring straight at Sandy.

Now the mind reader was saying, "I see something that ticks. I see something with hands. I see something that tells the time."

Sandy felt as if her heart had stopped.

The mind reader was asking Sandy to stand. Sandy stood up.

"I see a stolen watch in your right hand pocket," said the mind reader.

Sandy sighed, took the watch out of her pocket, and handed it to her uncle. "I'm sorry," she said.

Everyone clapped then, except for Sandy, because Sandy knew that the mind reader hadn't read her mind at all. The mind reader had *known* that Sandy had taken the watch.

How?

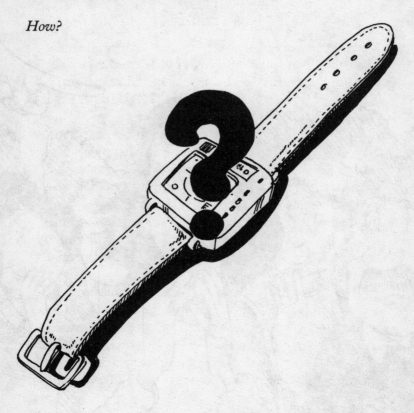

10. THE SECRET ROOM

Margaret saw the sign on the morning after the night they arrived at Hungry Lodge. She was standing in front of the bookcase in the library. The sign said, *DO NOT TOUCH THESE BOOKS.*

"Why not?" Margaret asked her father later.

"I'm not sure. I haven't been in there and I'm not going in there. But I think your uncle said something about a secret room behind the bookcase. He's like you. He likes puzzles, and mysteries, and secrets. But don't even *think* about trying to find it. When he gets here tomorrow he'll tell us all about it, so until then you must promise to stay away."

"I promise," Margaret said, crossing her fingers.

A secret room, now *that* was interesting. How could she possibly stay away from a secret room?

Later that night, after her parents had gone to bed, Margaret tiptoed into the library and turned on the light. She walked over to the bookcase and

studied it. She'd read a lot about secret rooms, and she knew that the door was always behind the bookcase, somewhere.

But where? There was probably a button behind one of the books that would move the bookcase, and then send the door creaking open so that she could climb in. But which book?

The left side of the bookcase was filled with encyclopaedias.

The middle was filled with history books. And the right section held novels. And... Wait. There was a mystery shelf. It was on the very bottom right-hand shelf. But there were only five mysteries on the shelf, which was odd. Why would someone buy an old creepy house like this one, with a secret room behind the bookcase, and only have five mysteries?

She looked at the titles. Moving from left to right, they were:

Margaret loved mysteries, and she wanted to read them all. But she had promised to stay away, hadn't she? Well, she *had* had her fingers crossed.

She took *The Secret Door* off the shelf first, and when she didn't find the button there, she went back to the beginning. She took the history books off first. One by one, she took them out, then returned them to where they had been. She was careful about that, because she didn't want anyone to know that she had been looking for that secret room, ever. There were no buttons behind the history books, which didn't surprise her. Secret buttons to secret rooms would be behind mysteries, wouldn't they?

She took the mysteries off the shelf, one at a time, until she came to the last one. And that is when she found the button.

Holding the book in one hand, she pushed the button with the other. The bookcase swayed, then flew open to reveal a small brown door with a large handle.

She wouldn't open it. She *would* open it. *No* – yes, no – *yes*. She slid the book between two other mysteries carefully, and turned the handle.

The door opened. It was very dark in there, too dark to see anything. She hesitated, took a deep breath, and stepped into the secret room – and as she did so the door slammed shut behind her and the bookcase slammed behind it.

It was terrifyingly quiet in the room, and terrifyingly dark. Margaret put her hands out in front of her and felt the darkness.

But there was nothing, and so she sat down on the floor and waited.

She thought about the mysteries. What were the titles? Something about a secret door, and Hungry Lodge. Hungry Lodge was the name of this place. That was strange. What were the others? *The Haunted Bookcase,* and *The Body in the Wall,* and *The Snake that Lived There.*

Someone would miss her soon. Someone would come and find her there, wouldn't they? But her father had said that he wouldn't go into the library, so maybe she'd have to stay there forever, in the haunted room with the body and the snake. There probably wasn't a snake there, or a body either. Was there? *Was* there?

No one came that night. Margaret sat in the dark secret room all night long and waited, thinking about bodies and snakes.

By morning she was convinced that they were there beside her and if she moved her foot or her hand she would feel them there.

How was she going to get out of there? No one knew that she was there, did they? Even her uncle wouldn't know when he came home, would he?

But he did. It must have been the next day, although she couldn't be sure of that. It was too dark. She heard them out there, on the other side of the bookcase. It was her father and her uncle, and they were saying something about her liking secrets, so maybe she had found her way into this one. She wanted to scream, but she couldn't. She couldn't make a sound. She was terrified that if there was a snake in the room, it would attack her. Wouldn't it? So she just sat there and hoped that they would find her.

"Well, well," she heard her uncle say. "I see that Margaret has found her way into my secret room. She did something that gave her away. Here, this is where the button is."

He pushed the button and the door flew open. He flashed the light round the secret room. Margaret opened her eyes.

"Are they there?" she whispered.

"Who?"

"The body. The snake. Are they there?"

Her uncle chuckled. "She always did have a good imagination," he said. "Like me, I guess. Come to think of it, maybe that's why I bought those five mysteries. To lead imaginative children like Margaret into adventures like this one."

Margaret looked around. The room was completely empty. She took a long, relieved breath, and then she scratched her head and wondered how they had found her. It must have had something to do with the books, she thought. But what?

What had Margaret done that showed her father and her uncle that she had discovered the secret door?

11. THE MYSTERY OF THE GHOSTLY FOOTSTEPS

The hotel that Nadia's family owned was so far away from any town that no one went there very much. The hotel was so old that sometimes, when the wind came up hard, the chimneys and windows could be heard to rattle a bit.

Nadia loved living in the old hotel, especially when strange guests came to stay. But at this particular time, no one very interesting was staying, and they had all been there for such a long time that Nadia had almost forgotten about them. There were Mr and Mrs Hopper, the old couple that had come for a week, and had stayed and stayed because Mr Hopper had broken his leg. Mr Hopper had recovered, but he still walked with a cane. Then there was William Pitt, the man who was writing a book about turtles and red ants. He had been there for six months and had only written two chapters so far. And there was the strange lady named Miss Pottle, who had been there so long that Nadia couldn't remember a time when she hadn't been there. Miss Pottle reminded Nadia of the old hotel. She was the same grey colour, and the sighs and creaks that she made sounded just like it.

The biggest problem with all these people was that they wouldn't believe her when she told them about the ghost. And an even bigger problem was the fact that none of them had ever even heard it.

Nadia heard the ghost for the first time on a dark and stormy night in January. William Pitt and Miss Pottle had already been there for several months, and Mr and Mrs Hopper had been there for two. Nadia was in her room, looking at her coin collection, when she heard a strange noise coming from the attic above her. The wind was blowing the old hotel with sudden deep breaths now, causing it to tremble and gasp in the black, black night. But Nadia knew that it was the ghost walking above her. She knew it because the wind did not move about the house like that, not with that soft, strange *step, slide, step, slide* sound.

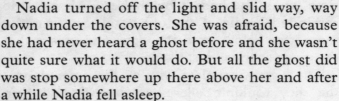

Nadia turned off the light and slid way, way down under the covers. She was afraid, because she had never heard a ghost before and she wasn't quite sure what it would do. But all the ghost did was stop somewhere up there above her and after a while Nadia fell asleep.

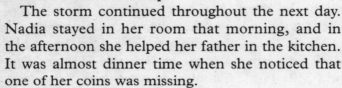

The storm continued throughout the next day. Nadia stayed in her room that morning, and in the afternoon she helped her father in the kitchen. It was almost dinner time when she noticed that one of her coins was missing.

That night the ghost walked again.

The next day another coin was missing, and the day after that another one had gone, and the ghost came and went, and came and went.

Nadia was convinced that the ghost had taken her coins, but when she told the others they wouldn't believe her. They didn't believe in ghosts, they said, especially ghosts that steal coins.

For the next few nights, Nadia stayed in her bed and thought about that, and she listened. The old hotel creaked and quivered under the weight of the wind, but the ghost, it seemed, had gone.

The next morning at breakfast, Nadia said, "You *must* have heard the ghost."

Everyone said that they hadn't. "Perhaps it's because the ghost only walks in the part of the attic above your room," Miss Pottle said.

"Or maybe it's in your dreams," said William Pitt.

"Ghosts in dreams don't take coins," Nadia insisted. "He's up there, I tell you. He's up there, waiting with my coins, and tonight I'll prove it. Come with me and I'll show you."

That night, shortly before eleven o'clock, the little group gathered at the foot of the stairs that led to the attic. Nadia led the way. As she climbed the dark narrow staircase that spiralled up, up, into the attic, she heard the others behind her. She could hear Miss Pottle's heavy breathing as she made her way up the staircase, and William Pitt's resigned sighs. She heard Mr Hopper drop his cane, and then she heard Mrs Hopper whisper, "Leave it."

They stopped at the top of the staircase. The attic was so dark that it was impossible to see anything at all, not each other, and not a ghost. But perhaps they could hear one, if they were very quiet.

They waited, and listened, but the ghost did not come. He did not come until Nadia began to move through the blackness, her arms stretched out in front of her. She was feeling for something, anything: the ghost perhaps, or maybe her coins.

And then she bumped into something, and she stopped, and felt that it was an old chest of some kind. Then, from somewhere behind her, came the sound of the ghost walking that strange *step slide, step slide* walk.

"Quick!" she cried. "Turn on the light."

William Pitt was the closest to the switch; he flipped it and the attic came alive with the light.

"You see," said Miss Pottle. "This is silly. There isn't a ghost here."

"I heard him!" Nadia said. "I know I did!"

Then she looked down and saw the chest. She opened it. It was filled with old silver and some antique ornaments, and right down at the bottom, her coins.

"You see," she said. "The ghost has been here."

One by one, the others came to the chest. Nadia heard them come up behind her, and when she heard that same strange *step slide* sound, she turned quickly, and faced the ghost.

But of course it wasn't a ghost at all. One of the guests had taken the coins and hidden them away, with the family silver, in the chest above her room.

Who was it?

12. THE HORROR FILM

There were four of them there in the third row. They had arrived early so they could sit right in the middle. They had each bought some crisps and sat down and opened them.

James was on the left, then Diane, then Omar. Mario was on the right. They had the perfect seats. No one was in front of them, and no one was behind them.

"It's supposed to be a scary film," Omar said, as he ate his last crisp and put the bag into his pocket.

It didn't start out very scary, but it got better and better as it went on.

It was about a reptile that grew longer and longer. It slid through a town, destroying buildings and people as it went.

"What's that?" Mario whispered, as the reptile slithered past a large building.

"It's the library," Omar said.

Suddenly the reptile's tail swung against the building.

Bricks and books and people sailed about.

James chomped his crisps nervously.

"Shhh!" Mario hissed.

James shoved his crisps into his pocket too.

The reptile was slithering onto Main Street now. It was puffing past the ice cream shop and huffing past the butcher's. Its tail swung back and forth, back and forth.

Diane opened her bag of crisps and devoured them in five minutes.

The reptile was passing the cinema now. It was stopping. It was going in.

The people inside the cinema were watching a scary film about a reptile that destroys a town.

James, Omar, Diane, and Mario were so enthralled that they barely blinked.

The reptile moved quietly this time. It did not make a sound. The people in the cinema were silent, too, as they leaned forward and stared in front of them.

And then there was a sound. It was just a little sound.

Someone in a seat behind them was opening a bag of crisps. But there was no one there. They had all looked a few minutes before, and the seats behind them were empty.

The reptile was moving closer and closer to the front of the theatre. He was moving into the fourth row. He was leaning over.

Suddenly Omar screamed, and then Diane screamed, and they both jumped up and screamed and screamed.

"It's there!" they screamed. "It's there! It's behind us. It tickled my leg. It grabbed my leg. I can't look. I can't look."

But they did look, and no one was there at all. There were no people in the row behind, and there was no reptile.

"But someone *did* tickle my leg!" Omar cried.

"And someone grabbed mine!" Diane said. Her voice was shaky and very soft.

On the screen, the reptile was being captured.

In the theatre, the culprit that grabbed and tickled their legs was being captured too.

"It was you!" Diane yelled at Omar.

"No," Omar said. "It must have been James."

"No way," James insisted. "But it *was* one of us, because no one else had time to get there. But which one?"

"I know," Diane said. "It's an open and shut case. He gave himself away."

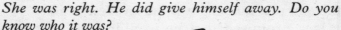

She was right. He did give himself away. Do you know who it was?

13. THE THING

Mr Gregory kicked the front door open and carried the ship over to the table. It was a beautiful ship, with delicate tiny riggings, and lovely little paper sails.

"It's a very old model," Mr Gregory explained to his son Jack. "And it's worth a lot of money. I'll take it down to the shop tomorrow morning, but in the meantime, don't touch it."

Mr Gregory owned an antique shop, and he often brought home lovely old things, but Jack thought that this ship was the loveliest of all.

Jack promised that he wouldn't go near the ship, but it was very hard for him, because he loved models more than anything.

He spent most of his time building model trains and model planes and model ships, and this model was the best one that he had ever seen.

When his father had gone to bed, Jack crept down again, went over to the ship and studied it.

At first he did not touch it, but after a while the temptation to stroke the tiny pieces of wood was too much.

He leaned over, then leaned back and looked behind him. The room was empty. He leaned over again and touched the rigging...until it broke.

It wasn't a very big piece. It was just a small bit of wood, but it was broken all the same.

Jack picked up the broken piece. Then he picked up the ship, and he carried them both up the stairs and into his room. He pushed the door closed gently, so as not to wake his parents, and carried the ship over to the table where he worked on his models.

He picked up his new jar of glue and read the label. *This powerful super-glue dries in ten minutes,* it said.

"Go to sleep, Jack," his father hollered. "Turn off the light, now, and go to sleep."

Jack laid the tiny piece of rigging on the table next to the opened jar of glue and flipped off the light. He climbed into bed, pulled the covers up to his chin, and waited for his parents to turn off the light in their room.

There was no moon that night, so Jack's room was very dark. He could see the light from his parents' room through the crack under his door but, except for that, there was no light in the room at all.

He waited for a long time, and just when he was drifting off to sleep he heard a sound, and then another, and another.

Something was in the room with him, and it was moving, slowly, around the room.

At first Jack thought that it was a mouse, but then he realized that it was bigger than that. He heard it scurrying across the room towards his bed, where it stopped, finally, and waited.

Jack pulled the covers up over his head and slid down towards the bottom of the bed. The thing shook, and tiptoed on across the room. Then it climbed up onto the windowsill, jumped from the windowsill, and landed on the table with a loud *thump!*

The thing shifted its weight. Next door the light went out in his parents' room. Jack held his breath and waited. The thing moved, then moved again, and tipped over the jar of glue.

Jack pushed back the covers and listened as the jar rolled around on the table and large blobs of glue fell to the floor. Except for the numbers *10:00* blinking on the digital clock, there was no light in the room at all.

Jack waited then, waited as if he was paralysed, as the numbers on the clock flashed...

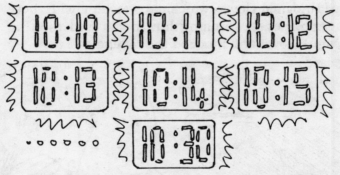

The thing moved then, and the rigging fell...and then the numbers flashed on and on, until they read *10:30*. Jack listened, waited, and after a moment he heard the thing shuffle to the edge of the table and leap onto the floor.

He leaned over and turned on the light by his bed. The thing was a huge brown rat with large teeth, a long, skinny tail, and glaring squinty eyes.

The rat was standing in the glue. It was not moving. It's stuck, Jack thought, stuck fast. If I go over there and find the rigging and take a little of the glue, I will be able to fix the rigging before the glue dries.

He slid out of bed and tiptoed across the floor.

The rat's eyes narrowed as Jack moved closer. Its tail quivered and its body shivered, but its legs did not move. Jack came to the rat and leaned over and saw, sticking out from under its belly, the piece of rigging.

"I'm safe," Jack thought. "The rat is stuck there. But maybe the rigging can be saved. I'll just give it a tiny little pull and..."

He leaned closer, watching, watching with those horrible eyes watching him back, and then he leaned down and touched the rigging and...

Suddenly the rat arched its back and lunged forward, scratching Jack's face. Jack ducked, moving his head to the right, and the rat catapulted past his shoulder and disappeared.

The next morning, when Mr Gregory came down for breakfast, the ship was exactly where he had left it the night before, and the rigging was fixed.

How could Jack have saved the rigging and repaired the ship? Jack thought *that the rat was stuck in the glue, so how was the rat able to lunge at Jack?*

14. THE HOWLING

Elena found the dog first. It was a funny little black mutt with funny little ears and a funny little tail that looked like it had been chopped off.

The mutt wandered into Elena's life one morning in the middle of the summer and it just stayed and stayed and stayed. Elena reported it to the police, and took out an ad in the paper, but no one claimed it, so she asked her parents if she could keep it. They agreed, as long as the dog was quiet and didn't bark.

She named the mutt Sam.

Elena had a best friend named Gillian who lived next door. When Gillian saw Sam she said, "That's my dog. It spent the night at my house a few weeks ago."

"His name is Sam," Elena said. "And he's mine. He'll be my dog forever." Then she mumbled something.

"What?" Gillian asked.

"As long as he doesn't bark," Elena said, louder.

Gillian glared. "He's mine," she hissed.

Sam followed Elena everywhere. He slept on the bottom of her bed and never made a sound when she was sleeping. And he tried very, very hard not to bark.

And then the howling began.

It started one night in July when there was a full moon. Sam heard it first. He sat up, cocked his little ears up high, and listened. And then he began to bark.

"Shhh," Elena whispered, but Sam wouldn't stop.

"Be quiet!" Elena said, giving him a little nudge.

Sam went quiet, but the howling continued. It was coming from far away. It sounded like a wolf.

When Gillian came over the next day, Elena told her about the wolf.

That night the howling began right after Elena and Sam had gone to sleep. It was a black, black night, and there was no moon, so when Sam began to bark it took Elena a moment to find him and silence him.

When he was finally quiet, she lay back on her pillow and listened. The howling seemed closer this time, and a bit louder, as if the wolf was moving in.

The next night it was closer still. This time, when Sam barked, Elena's father called out to her. "If he isn't quiet he'll have to go," he shouted.

Elena covered Sam with the covers so that if he barked it wouldn't sound so loud. They fell asleep like that, and the only noise was the sound of Elena's soft breathing and Sam's light snoring.

The wolf woke them. Elena opened her eyes, rubbed them, and placed her hand gently over Sam's mouth so that he wouldn't bark.

She heard the wolf moaning, moaning. It was moving closer, through the bushes, and across the garden. Then it stopped next to the tree that grew outside her window.

Sam gave a quick, frightened bark. Then he stopped, gazed up at Elena in the dark, and waited. He had learned. He understood now that he was to be quiet.

They waited together, shivering under the blankets. Outside, the growing wind shook the tree. The wolf howled. He was there, under her open window.

Do wolves climb trees? Elena wondered. Outside, the wolf howled again.

And then the storm began. The wind came up and the rain began to fall, followed by a loud, moaning howl. He was still there, under her window, waiting.

I should close my window, Elena thought. But what if he's out there? What if he's climbed the tree? What if he grabs me when I try and close it?

She pushed Sam away then, and slid out of bed. The winds were stronger now, and loud crashes of thunder rolled through the sky.

From somewhere in the branches came the sound of the wolf howling, howling. The rain was pouring in now, drenching the room. He howled again. He was in the tree, but lower than the window. It would take her about thirty seconds to run to the window and close it. Thirty seconds. Would he be able to climb the rest of the way in thirty seconds?

She turned. Behind her, Sam was watching, waiting.

Thirty seconds, no, twenty now. She took a breath, then ran, no, *raced*, towards the window and slammed it shut. Outside, the rain stopped, suddenly.

Shutting the window made her feel brave enough to go after the wolf. She wasn't afraid of him any more. She tiptoed out of her room. Sam followed, quietly. They moved together silently, down the stairs, and outside, to the tree.

Something was up there. Elena could hear it, but she couldn't see it. It would have to come down, sometime, and so she would wait. It did not take long.

It came down slowly, shaking the branches, and oozed into the mud below. It was Gillian.

"I heard it howling," Gillian said. "And I heard Sam barking. So I came to help. I saw the wolf climb the tree, and I climbed after it. I chased it down and scared it away. It ran off, just now."

"After the rain?" Elena asked.

Gillian nodded. "That's right."

"I wonder," Elena said, and then she and Sam searched around the tree together. They were looking for something, but it wasn't there.

"You're lying," Elena said. "If a wolf runs off right after a rainstorm it leaves something behind. There wasn't a wolf anywhere near here. You make a good wolf, Gillian, but not good enough. Wolves are more clever. You can lead a dog to a wolf, but you can't make him bark. This dog is staying right here, with me."

What would a wolf leave behind after a rainstorm?

15. THE DUMMY

Adam Alexander rose from his chair and bowed. Someone clapped, and then more people clapped, and then more, and more, until the room was loud with clapping. Adam smiled and clutched his dummy closer to him.

"They like us, Martin," Adam whispered. "They *really* like us."

Adam was partially right. The audience liked Adam, but they *loved* Martin. Adam was a nice boy, but Martin was wonderful.

Everyone loved Martin. They said he was sweet. They said he looked so real, with that red hair and those soft blue eyes. He was almost human, they said. Not like a dummy at all.

Of course, the reason that Martin seemed real was because Adam was such a good ventriloquist. He made sure that Martin was the one that said funny things. He moved Martin's head just a bit when Martin was speaking. And, most important, he never moved his lips when he threw his voice.

Yes, Adam was a very good ventriloquist indeed.

But on this particular day, Adam was something else as well. He was an accomplice to a robbery. That evening, on the way to the show, he had watched as Henry took £500 from the cash register in the front of Mrs Brannon's video shop. Henry was a boarder in his house, and Adam didn't know him very well, but he never would have guessed that Henry was a thief.

And now Adam was an accomplice, just because he had been there, beside him.

Adam bowed again and carried Martin off the stage. He tucked Martin into his suitcase gently and took him home.

The house was dark, and Adam was glad about that. He wanted to be alone for a while so he could think about whether to turn Henry in.

He carried Martin into the house, flipped on a light, took a small key from his trousers pocket, and unlocked the cupboard by the front door.

He slid the suitcase into the cupboard, closed and locked the cupboard door, and went into the kitchen to make some tea.

Fifteen minutes later, while he was pouring his tea in the sitting room, the doorbell rang.

A policeman was at the door.

"Adam Alexander?" the policeman said.

Adam nodded.

"I'm afraid you're in a bit of trouble. A Mrs Brannon at the video shop says she saw you take some money from her cash register."

"Me? She saw *me* take it?"

"That's right," the policeman said.

"Just me?"

"Just you. She said you were carrying a suitcase."

"She didn't see anyone else?" Adam asked.

The policeman folded his arms and looked down at Adam suspiciously.

"Why?" he asked. "Was someone else there?"

Adam shook his head quickly, shrugged, and

said, "No. No. I was, uh, just wondering." He wasn't ready to tell on Henry.

Not yet.

"Mind if I look around?" the policeman asked.

Adam shrugged and waited as the policeman opened and closed doors and looked in cupboards. Adam knew he was looking for the money, and he was glad that it wasn't in the house. He guessed that Henry had it in his pocket.

"It's locked," the policeman said, as he turned the handle of the front cupboard door.

Adam reached into his pocket, pulled out the key, and handed it to him.

The policeman unlocked the door and rummaged through the clothes. For some reason he didn't seem especially interested in the suitcase on the floor, or maybe he just didn't notice it. When he had finished he closed and locked the door and slipped the key into his pocket.

Adam followed him into the sitting room and offered him some tea.

They were drinking their tea when the laughter began. At first it was muffled and hard to hear, but soon it grew louder, then louder still.

Adam froze. The laughter was coming from the cupboard. It was Martin's laugh. Yes, it was Martin.

The laughter grew strange then. It was as if Martin had gone a little mad. The laughter sounded sinister and rather weird. Martin was chuckling, as if he was about to do something terrible.

The policeman put down his cup and looked over at Adam. "That's very good," he said.

"What is?" Adam asked.

"The way you can throw your voice like that. I've seen your show, and I know you're a very good ventriloquist for your age, but I didn't know you could do that."

"Do what?"

"Throw your voice all the way to the cupboard like that. *And* while you're drinking tea, too."

"Oh," was all that Adam could think to say. Adam was as surprised as the policeman, because he hadn't been throwing his voice at all.

Neither of them said anything for several minutes, and then that strange chuckling began again. The policeman was studying Adam carefully now, and Adam knew that he was trying to see if his lips were moving.

And then Martin started to speak.

"Adam, Adam let me out," he said. "Adam, Adam let me out. Or I will tell him all about..." Martin stopped suddenly. The room was eerily silent.

The policeman broke the silence. "That was very, very good," he said.

Adam was trying to think of something to say when Martin spoke again.

"I will tell him all about how you took the money today," Martin shouted.

The policeman's eyes widened and he put his cup on the table and stood up.

"Odd that you should have him say that," he said.

Adam couldn't speak. All he could do was sit there in his chair and tremble, and wait.

Martin began again. "You shouldn't steal things, Adam, dear. Or hide the stolen money here. Take me out. Take me out. Take me out or I'll count to three, and pull this money out of me." And then that weird creepy chuckling echoed throughout the room.

The policeman was frowning at Adam now. "I don't understand why you would have him say that," he said. "Unless you're feeling guilty. That can be the only reason you're helping him to accuse you. He may have been a witness, of course, but a dummy can't testify in court. Of course, he won't need to testify if the money's *really* inside him. That's all the evidence we'll need."

"I didn't do it!" Adam cried then. "I mean it. It was someone else. And I didn't throw my voice then either. That was someone else too, someone who must have been listening to me practice. They must have learnt how to do Martin's voice. Someone else took that money, and someone else was making Martin talk."

The policeman just looked at him.

The policeman stood then, and went towards the cupboard. He turned the handle of the door, pulled it open and slid out the suitcase. He took out Martin, pulled off his head, reached inside and took out the £500.

"What – " gasped Adam.

"I guess that's it, then," the policeman said.

"It wasn't me," Adam insisted. "It was someone else."

"Who?" asked the policeman.

The front door opened and Henry walked in. "There he is now," Adam said.

"You've just been accused of robbery," the policeman told Henry.

"Oh, really?" Henry said. "And what did I steal?"

"£500," the policeman said.

"And did you recover the money?" Henry asked.

"It was in the dummy," the policeman told him. "Adam admitted it just now. Well, Martin blew the whistle on him, but it was Adam speaking, of course."

Henry smirked and said, "Well, that's proves it. It's Adam's dummy."

"Someone else was in that cupboard!" Adam cried. "There must have been."

The policeman paced back and forth for a while, and when he had finished pacing he said, "Yes. Yes, of course. Someone *was* in that cupboard, and it wasn't you, Adam. Empty your pockets, Henry, and we'll see if it could have been you."

Henry emptied his pockets and gave himself away. How?

16. THE GHOSTLY MESSAGE

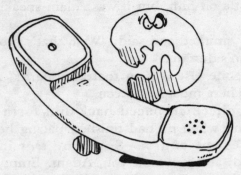

Danielle's mother went to bed at nine o'clock on the night of the ghostly message. Before she went to bed, she said, "If the phone rings, please answer it. And take a message."

The phone rang an hour later.

"The money is under the fifth sycamore," a voice said.

"I'm sorry?" Danielle said.

The man hesitated, and then he said "Oh, wrong number," and hung up.

Danielle put the receiver down and went back into the sitting room. She tried to concentrate on her book but she couldn't. She kept thinking about the message. *What* money? *What* fifth sycamore?

The phone rang again an hour later.

"Is this Linda?" the same voice asked after she had said hello.

"No, it's Danielle. Where is the fifth sycamore?" But then she felt nervous, and she hung up. There

are sycamores everywhere, Danielle thought.
They were all over town, and all over the world.

The fifth sycamore might even be in France.

The phone rang once more that night. Danielle
wasn't sure if she should answer it, but she was
curious about the money and so she did.

"If you tell anyone about the money you'll be
very sorry," hissed the same voice.

Danielle slammed the phone down.

She didn't sleep at all that night. She kept thinking about all that money buried under that sycamore tree.

She got up very early the next morning and went outside. She touched a sycamore tree, and then she touched another, and another. But she knew she was being silly, and so she went back inside.

While she was eating breakfast someone knocked on the front door. Danielle's mother went to answer it.

"I'm here to fix the phone," a voice said.

"Is something wrong with it?" her mother asked.

"All the phones in town have been out all night," the voice said.

They came into the kitchen then, and the man went over to the phone. Danielle put down her cereal spoon.

"What time did the phones go out?" she asked.

"Eat your breakfast dear," her mother said.

"Nine o'clock." The man put the receiver to his ear and listened. "It's fine," he said.

"Well, our phone wasn't out," Danielle insisted. "Someone called at ten."

"Eat your cereal, pet," her mother said.

The man chuckled. "That's impossible, Danielle," he said. "You could have dreamt it. Or perhaps it was a ghost calling."

Danielle's mother led the man out of the kitchen. "She has a vivid imagination," Danielle heard her say. And then the front door slammed and her mother came back into the kitchen.

"You must have had a bad dream," her mother said.

"I didn't!" Danielle cried. "And it wasn't a ghost either. That man wants me to *think* I was dreaming. He wants me to think it was a ghost. But it wasn't. That was the man who called last night. He said something that gave him away." Danielle whispered a word into her mother's ear and her mother nodded. The man had indeed said something that only the caller could have known.

When she was sure that her mother believed her, Danielle went over to the window. The man was climbing into the front of a blue van. Danielle wrote down the licence number, and then she dialled the police.

"If you hurry you'll catch a thief," she said. "And the money is hidden under the fifth sycamore tree."

She gave the police the licence number and hung up.

The police were in time. The phone man was really a thief, as Danielle had said. And the man told them that the money was under the fifth sycamore tree on a lane fifty miles away.

The police wondered how the phone man had given himself away.

What word did he say that gave him away?

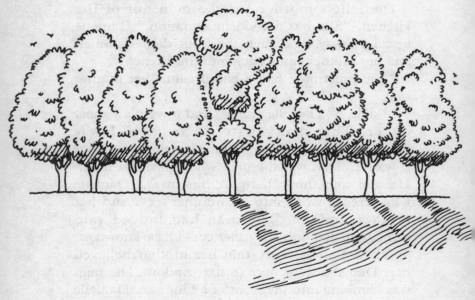

17. LOST!

Once in a while Amanda Jane's imagination got the best of her. She was a very, very smart girl and when she wasn't reading or writing stories or learning a new language she was imagining. And sometimes the things that she imagined scared her out of her wits.

Now, when Amanda wasn't imagining, she was solving problems. Amanda loved to solve problems. She loved chess, and maths, and she especially liked maze puzzles.

Amanda did a maze every single day of her life. One Saturday she said to her friends, Diane and Helen, "I have just finished the most difficult maze in my maze book *The Ten Most Difficult Mazes in the World*. Now I think that I'd like to try and find my way through a *real* maze, the kind that's cut out of bushes, that you can walk around in. In fact, I would like to try and get through the most difficult *real* maze in the world." Then she rolled up her maze book and shoved it into her pack.

"Well, the hardest maze is at Netherden, about one hour away," said Helen. "You'll have to take the bus."

"Let's go now," Amanda said. "And I'll bet you that I can get through that maze in ten minutes."

"That's impossible," Diane said.

It was a pleasant, sunny day, and the girls all agreed to go to the maze, but neither of the others wanted to go through the maze. It was such a difficult maze that people had been known to be caught in it for days and days and nights and nights.

"You'll have to go alone," Diane and Helen said· to Amanda. "We'll wait for you at the other end."

"I'll be out in ten minutes," Amanda assured them, and everybody laughed.

"Bet?" Amanda said.

"Bet," the girls agreed. "Bet you a pound between all of us that you can't."

Amanda handed her pack to Helen to look after, waved, and ran into the maze. Her friends waved and then they began to walk round to the back of the maze. They walked slowly, because they didn't think that Amanda could make it through in ten minutes – but when they arrived she was already there.

"It was easy," she said.

Diane and Helen knew that something was fishy, but no one quite understood what it was. "You've been here before," Diane said.

Amanda said that she hadn't. And she was telling the truth.

The girls paid up, and then Diane said, "If you can get through the maze in ten minutes, you should be able to go back the other way in five. Even though it *is* going to rain."

Amanda looked up at the dark sky and shook her head. "Maybe another day," she said.

"It's not going to rain in the next five minutes," Helen said. "You can make it."

Amanda didn't want to go, but they dared her and dared her until she finally went. As she started in they heard her whisper, "Maybe if I just turn it over," which seemed a bit puzzling.

Diane and Helen ran round to the front of the maze and waited.

Inside the maze, Amanda was having trouble. She was trying to tell herself that she could do it. She kept thinking, turn it upside down. Turn it upside down. If you can do it one way, then you can do it upside down.

But she couldn't. She kept turning right when she should have turned left, and before she knew it she was circling round and round and back and forth in the tall bushes and the sky was growing darker and darker.

It was then that her imagination shifted into full power. She started to pretend that she was in a jungle and she had to get out. She didn't want to pretend that, but she didn't have any choice.

It just happened. She began to imagine there were tigers behind every bush and lions around

every corner. She saw cobras in the bushes and heard wild boar behind her. There was nowhere that she could turn or move or hide, and so she stopped, and stayed there, terrified.

The sky was darker now, and the rain was starting to fall. The lions and the tigers were hungry, and the snakes were waiting.

Thunder shook the bushes, and Amanda froze, and started to cry.

No-one would come. No-one would go through a maze in the rain. And Diane and Helen wouldn't be able to find her, because they didn't know anything about mazes.

But Amanda was wrong. Her friends knew enough about mazes to know that it is impossible to get through the hardest one in the world in ten minutes, no matter who you are. So while Amanda was fighting off the animals in the jungle, they were thinking, and thinking, and thinking, until they figured out how Amanda had done it. And when they turned it upside down they were able to go in and rescue her from the lions.

How were Diane and Helen able to get through the maze and rescue Amanda, quickly?

18. THE HOUSE OF HORRORS

The first bolt of lightning shot through the sky just as Oliver, Elena, and Ben were climbing out of the front seat on the roller coaster.

Thunder followed, and then another bolt of lightning, then more, and more thunder. They knew they were in for it.

"The park's closing anyway," Ben shouted. "We should go home."

They tried. They ran as fast as they could towards the bus stop, but the sky grew dark and the first drops of rain hit them before they were half way through the park. It was going to be a bad, bad storm.

"What are we going to do?" Oliver asked.

Elena looked around, noticed the House of Horrors, and said, "How about in there? It's still open."

And indeed it was. The old man who watched over it was around the side, talking to some children, but the door was wide open.

Elena and Oliver raced through the doorway. When they were safely inside they turned, and waited, as the skies opened, and the rain poured down. Ben saw them there and ran through the puddles to them as the rain soaked through his clothes.

"It's a bit, uh, dark in here," Oliver whispered.

"It's even darker way inside," Elena whispered back. "Have you ever been in there?"

"No," said a voice in the darkness.

"Well, I have," Elena told them. "And it's very, very dark, and very, very creepy."

Just then the door slammed behind them, and someone, probably the old man, turned the key from the outside, locking the door.

"*Hey!*" Oliver cried. But no one answered.

"*WE'RE STILL IN HERE!*" Ben hollered.

The old man was gone now, to his home, and his wife, and his dinner. He was not thinking about the House of Horrors at all.

Inside the spook house, Elena, Oliver, and Ben were trying to find each other. There was nothing there, nothing but blackness and the sounds of their voices.

"Is anybody there?" Oliver whispered.

"I'm here," Elena said. "But I wish I wasn't."

"How are we going to get out of here?" Ben said.

"There's a back door," Elena told him. "But we have to go all the way through to get there. Maybe there's a light switch."

They ran their fingers along the clammy damp walls, and when they couldn't find a switch, Elena said, "Follow me. I think I can find my way to the back door."

They moved through the cold blackness slowly, feeling the walls as they went. Elena knew what lay ahead, but she didn't know when.

Behind her, someone hit the button that started that hysterical, terrifying laughter that Elena knew so well.

The laughter screamed and echoed around them, filling the gloom. She knew where they were now, because she had hit that button before, and heard that laughter before, and felt this terror before.

"Who pushed the button?" Elena whispered when the laughter died down.

"I didn't," Oliver and Ben said together.

"Well, someone did," Elena said.

Elena moved quietly this time, almost tiptoing. She was listening. She knew the whispers would start soon, assuming someone hit the whisper button. But there was no one in there, except the three of them, and she was the only one who knew where it was. She decided that she wouldn't hit it.

The whispers began about ten seconds after she had passed the switch. They were horrible. They started off softly, then grew louder and louder, until they surrounded her. It was as if the whole world was talking about her. She covered her ears, and finally they stopped.

From somewhere behind her came the sound of loud squishy footsteps.

The footsteps were right next to the whisper button.

"Who's there?" Elena called.

"Me," Oliver called back.

"Me too," Ben hollered.

"I wonder," Elena said.

Elena moved on. Behind her, the squishy footsteps moved closer. Elena stopped. She knew where the skeleton button was, but she wasn't going to push it, not this time. She wondered if whoever was following her would push it. She knew that Ben and Oliver wouldn't because they'd never been in here before. She moved on. The footsteps followed.

Suddenly the skeleton came alive. The bones lit up, jumping and dancing, and from the mouth of the skull came the sounds of pain.

The groans were horrible.

"Did you push it?" Elena whispered. She knew who she was talking to. She was talking to the footsteps.

"No," Oliver and Ben whispered back, their voices shaking nervously.

They turned a corner then, and came out into the light.

The light was coming from a window next to the back door.

When they saw each other they did not speak. They just looked at each other with wide, slightly frightened, slightly relieved eyes. Then, one by one, they tried the back door. It was locked.

"Break the window!" Elena called. "Break the window. Hurry, before the squishy footsteps get to us."

Ben broke the window and climbed out first. The old man must have heard him from his home next door, for he came out of his front door then and ran over.

"What do you think you're doing?" he cried. "This place is closed. Was it you making all that noise?"

"It wasn't us," Elena said. "We didn't push the buttons. It was somebody else. It was the person with the squishy footsteps."

"We'll see," said the old man, and then he searched the House of Horrors from top to bottom. There was nobody there at all.

"So one of you must have caused all this screeching and whispering and screaming," said the old man.

"Well, I'm the only one who's been here before," Elena explained. "And I didn't do it."

"Somebody's lying," said the old man. "Somebody else has been here enough times to know where all those buttons are. And I know who it is."

Do you? Who pushed the buttons?

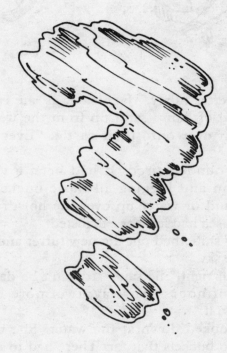

19. THE CAVE

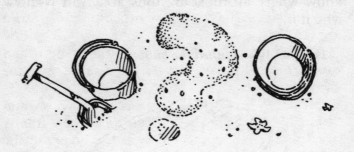

"We'd better hurry," Jane said, as she carried a bucketful of damp sand up from the water and turned it over onto their castle. "Everybody's gone."

Jane sounded tired. It had been a very hot afternoon and lugging all those bucketfuls of damp sand or water up over the hot dry beach from the sea had left her exhausted.

Randy smoothed out the new turret and looked up at the sky.

"It's all right," he said. "It won't be dark for a couple of hours. Anyway, two more buckets should do it."

Jane looked down at the water. She couldn't carry two buckets that far. There had to be some damp sand somewhere closer.

The beach was so dry that it took her a long time to find the damp sand. And she was so tired that she had to put the buckets full of damp sand down every few steps and catch her breath.

By the time she returned the sky had turned a dark, dark grey and the sun had disappeared. Suddenly, the waves were churning and twisting and growing big as the wind moaned around them.

Randy stood up. "This is going to be a bad storm," he said. "We should get inside – into the cave!"

"Hurry," Jane cried. She was scared now, and she sounded as if she was going to cry. Randy tried to comfort her, for he was the bigger of the two, but it wasn't much use.

They began to run, but the wind blew harder and harder, until they could barely walk.

Jane led the way. It was hard going through the soft dry sand and the gusts of wind. At last she reached the cliff, and the cave, put down her buckets and turned to urge Randy on.

Once they were inside, looking out of the opening, Randy began to laugh. "Now *this* is fun," he said. "It's sort of like watching a film."

He was right. The cave was pitch black, like a cinema, and watching the storm was like looking at a screen.

The sky was darker now, and the waves were growing higher as they rolled up the beach towards them. The wind was building, too.

Inside the cave, the air was still. Jane and Randy sat together by the entrance and looked out.

"Randy?" Jane said, after a minute.

"Hmmm?"

"The tide's coming in." Jane was beginning to sound very nervous.

"It's all right," Randy said. Now that they were inside the cave they would be safe. Wouldn't they?

Even if they had to wait out the storm for a whole night they would be all right. Wouldn't they?

The tide was rolling in faster now. Jane wanted to make a run for it, but Randy knew better. The tide was too high. They wouldn't make it.

Most of the beach had gone now. The tide had hidden it, taking with it the tiny shells and the sandcastle and most of the footprints. There were a few sets left, including their own. But what were those strange ones that led past them, deep into the shadows of the cave? The prints were damp, as if they had just been made.

Randy wondered who, or what, they belonged to.

They were round, like huge, oversized hoofs... and they only led one way.

Someone, or something, must be in that cave with them.

"Hello!" Randy cried. But no one answered.

"Why are you doing that?" Jane whispered.

"Because something else is in here, Jane."

"Some*thing?*" Jane cried.

"HELLO! HELLO!" Randy hollered. His words echoed, but he knew that they were his own words and no one else's.

The water was rushing now, pushing and swirling and churning closer and closer to the cave.

"We'd better get out of here," Randy whispered. "But I don't know how."

Jane looked up at him with eyes filled with terror, and he wished that he hadn't said it. He had to make her think that they were going to be all right.

"Don't be scared," Randy said. But he was scared too, scared of being in a cave with an unseen something when the ocean kept moving closer and closer.

The next wave burst through the opening, spraying them. They jumped backwards and peered at each other through the darkness.

Randy took Jane's hand and led her deeper and deeper into the black cave, until they came to a rock wall and they stopped.

The water was up to their ankles now.

They had to get out of there. But how? There was no way out. There were nooks and crannies in caves, but they didn't have back doors. Or did they?

And what about those strange footprints? If that huge hoofed creature was in there, then... Randy couldn't bear to think about it.

And if *it* wasn't in there... *maybe* there was another way out...

"The water is up to my knees," Jane cried.

"I know, I know. But listen. Maybe there's a way out the back. I want you to raise your arms out to the sides and follow me back through the cave. Try and touch the walls on either side as you move, and I'll do the same. The cave is narrow so that shouldn't be hard. And Jane...."

"The water's touching my swimming costume," Jane said. Her voice sounded shaky and very scared.

"We have to hurry. But Jane, if you touch someone or something and it groans, or growls, promise that you'll try very hard not to scream, even if you're terrified," Randy said.

Jane whimpered.

They moved back, back, through the black cave like that, with their arms out at their sides. The damp walls felt clammy and cold under their fingertips.

"The water's coming!" Jane whispered once, as a big wave burst into the cave. "The water's coming."

"Hurry Jane, hurry. There must be a way out. I know there is. There just has to be."

They moved faster, faster, as the water grew higher behind them, until they were at the back wall of the cave and there was nowhere else to go.

"Did you feel anything?" Randy shouted above the roar of the water.

But Jane couldn't answer. She just kept repeating the same thing, over and over. "The water is coming. The water is coming."

Randy felt to his right. He felt another opening, grabbed Jane's hand, and pulled her as fast as he could until, at last, he saw the light. It was coming from the back of the cave. Suddenly, Randy wasn't afraid any more.

They followed the light until they came to an opening, and when they were through it and outside Jane started to cry.

"Don't cry," Randy said. "We're safe now. We can run home from here. And there wasn't anything in the cave. I know that now."

How did Randy know? Can you guess how the strange footprints leading up to the cave got there?

20. THE GHOST OF GREENFIELD MANOR

The Crawford twins did not want to move. They loved Greenfield Manor and the woods that surrounded it and the lake nearby and all their friends. The Crawford twins were determined to stay, no matter what their parents had in mind.

Their parents had something else in mind entirely. They were tired of Greenfield Manor. It was costing too much money and they wanted to sell it. In fact, it was almost sold. A pleasant young couple named Stanhope had agreed to their price and they were stopping by that very evening to sign the papers. Unless the Crawford twins could think of something... fast.

"I have a plan," Oliver Crawford told his sister as they came in from school. "Mum and Dad are coming home at eight, and the Stanhopes are arriving at nine. We'll call the Stanhopes and tell them to come at seven and then we'll haunt them out of our lives."

"I like that idea," said Tina Crawford.

Oliver and Tina locked the front door and went over to the table by the staircase. There was a white cloth on the table and Tina smiled when she saw it. It had been a year since she had spilled something on that cloth, and the stain was still there, under the phone. She picked up the receiver. There was no one in the house except Oliver, so she didn't even have to be quiet about their plan. Mrs Stanhope said she thought seven would be fine. Tina hung up the phone and followed Oliver upstairs to get ready.

Everything was ready when the front doorbell chimed at seven. The lights were dim and the twins were dressed for haunting.

"Come in!" Tina called from upstairs.

The twins heard somebody rattling around near the door latch and then the door squeaked slowly open.

"Go into the sitting room," Oliver shouted. "Our parents will be down in a minute."

They waited for ten minutes, until the Stanhopes had a chance to get settled in the sitting room, and then the haunting began.

The twins clomped about and squeaked and moaned and groaned in the room above the sitting room, and then they sneaked downstairs, making "Whoooing" noises in the hall, and turning off the lights as they went. At the sitting room door, Oliver reached in and flicked off the light switch, and then they squeaked the door open very slowly.

They knew that the Stanhopes were scared, because they didn't say a word. They were probably so scared that they wouldn't buy the house now and no one would have to move anywhere, ever. If they weren't scared now they would be in a few minutes.

Oliver and Tina held their white sheets tighter around them and floated into the sitting room. They couldn't see the Stanhopes but they could hear them breathing in the shadows by the chair in the corner.

Across the room, moonlight crept through the big windows.

Tina and Oliver moved towards it, and danced in it.

The Stanhopes must be so scared by now that they will be ready to leave... for ever, Tina thought.

They moved from the windows then, and floated from the room.

When they reached the door, they turned and peeked into the shadowy room to see if the Stanhopes were ready to flee yet. But what they saw instead was something white emerging from the chair in the corner. It rose up, larger and larger, and floated towards them, coming closer and closer, until it was almost beside them.

"A *ghost!*" cried Tina.

The twins turned and ran, down the hall, past the telephone table that used to have a white cloth on it, out the open front door, and into the night.

When they finally returned an hour later, their father was in the sitting room with the Stanhopes. He looked up, saw them, and chuckled.

"You don't want to buy this house," Tina told the Stanhopes. Her voice was trembling violently. "It's haunted. I mean, it's *really* haunted."

"Is it?" Mrs Stanhope asked. "How interesting."

Mr Crawford laughed and turned to the Stanhopes. "Let me explain," he said. "After you called me at the office to see if seven o'clock was all right, I knew something was up. So I came home early, and when I heard these two upstairs trying to haunt you out, I grabbed the cloth from the telephone table and gave them a bit of their own medicine. But they should have known it couldn't have been you in the sitting room. A *bell* should have given them the *key* when they heard all that *rattling*."

The Stanhopes couldn't possibly have been in the sitting room when all that haunting was going on. Why not?

ANSWERS

1 One Sausage Pizza, Two Pieces with Mushrooms

The first delivery man ate it. He was the only one who had a chance.

2   The Case of the Horrible Fingerprint

Jane always cracked her gum. After she took the charm, Jane stuck it under the table with her gum, so that she could retrieve it later.

3   The Thirteenth Floor

Sophie said that she took the lift to the 13th floor, and then she took it again, down to the 12th floor. But Tim only heard the elevator doors open and close *once*. Since it was such an old elevator, he surely would have heard the doors if they had opened a second time.

4 The Goldfish

When Mark pulled the plug to let the spider out he "shoved his sleeve down into the water". His wet sleeve reminded him of his sister's damp cuff . . . just damp enough to have taken a small goldfish out of a bath.

5 A Night on the Big Wheel

It had to be the man with the red hat, because he was seated directly below Angela and Edmond. Everyone else had climbed off and had left when the man in the red hat got off and tied up the operator. Angela and Edmond were left, of course, on the very top.

6   The Spider That Wouldn't Die

The web wasn't growing any larger. If the same spider had been growing and growing, then the web would have grown, too.

7   The Tap on the Window

The boy himself had been causing the tapping. He was blind. He had been dreaming that something was tapping on his window, and he was screaming and walking in his sleep. The tapping sound was caused by his own cane.

8 The Scavenger Hunt

The mirror was intact when Jamie left the house. Jamie broke the mirror when he slammed the door and went out.

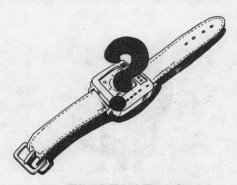

9 The Mind Reader

The mind reader didn't have to read Sandy's mind because she already knew all about the watch. The mind reader was Jill.

10 The Secret Room

The books were in alphabetical order according to author. Margaret took the last mystery off the shelf, then "slid the book between two other mysteries". The books were no longer in alphabetical order, making it obvious that she had been there.

11 The Mystery of the Ghostly Footsteps

Mr Hopper had broken his leg. He dragged his leg, making a *step, slide* sound. He was the culprit who was pilfering Nadia's coins.

12   The Horror Film

Mario was the culprit. He was the only one of the
four who hadn't opened his crisps before someone
opened a bag in the row behind.

13   The Thing

The label on the glue said "This powerful super
glue dries in ten minutes". The glue was already
dry when the rigging *and* the rat landed on it.

14 The Howling

Wolves leave footprints behind. The only
footprints under the tree belonged to Gillian.
Gillian was trying to get Sam to bark so that she
could have him.

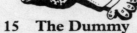

15 The Dummy

Adam couldn't have been in the cupboard because
he was with the policeman the whole time. The
policeman had locked the cupboard door after he
had investigated it, but it was unlocked the second
time he opened it. Dummys in suitcases can't
unlock doors. Henry had another key to the
cupboard – and it was in his pocket.

16 The Ghostly Message

The phone man said the word, "Danielle". No-one had mentioned Danielle's name except Danielle herself, when she talked to him the night before . . . on the phone.

17 Lost!

Her friends had Amanda's pack, and inside it was her book of mazes. This maze, the maze that Amanda was inside right at that moment, was in that book, and if they "turned it upside down" they could go through the maze the other way and rescue Amanda. Amanda hadn't been in that maze before, but she had pencilled her way through it in the book.

18   The House of Horrors

The squishy footsteps belonged to Ben. He was the only one to come in *after* the real downpour started – and he ran through a puddle.

19   The Cave

Jane's two heavy pails made the sets of round prints when she stopped to rest. She had forgotten that.

20 The Ghost of Greenfield Manor

Oliver and Tina locked the front door when they came home from school. When the doorbell chimed Tina called "Come in!" from upstairs. They heard "rattling" and then the door squeaked open. No one could have come in without a key. It was Mr Crawford who arrived at seven and rattled his keys.